Alphabeasts

**To my mother — thank you for encouraging
the modest talents of your little boy.**

To my love, Katie — thank you for encouraging me in my work.

Text and illustrations © 2002 Wallace Edwards

Kids Can Press acknowledges the financial support of the Ontario Arts Council,
the Canada Council for the Arts and the Government of Canada, through
the BPIDP, for our publishing activity.

Published in Canada by
Kids Can Press Ltd.
29 Birch Avenue
Toronto, ON M4V 1E2

Published in the U.S. by
Kids Can Press Ltd.
2250 Military Road
Tonawanda, NY 14150

www.kidscanpress.com

The artwork in this book was rendered
in watercolor and colored pencil.
The text is set in Giovanni Book.

Edited by Tara Walker
Designed by Julia Naimska
Printed in Hong Kong, China,
by Book Art Inc., Toronto

This book is smyth sewn casebound.

CM 02 0 9 8 7 6 5 4

National Library of Canada Cataloguing in Publication Data

Edwards, Wallace
Alphabeasts

ISBN 1-55337-386-3

1. English language — Alphabet — Juvenile literature.
2. Animals — Juvenile literature. I. Title.

PE1155.E38 2002   j421'.1   C2001-903689-2

Kids Can Press is a **corus**™ Entertainment company

Alphabeasts

Wallace Edwards

Kids Can Press

A is for Alligator,
awake from a dream.

B is for Bat,
slurping ice cream.

C is for Cat,
who reflects on its self.

D is for Duck,
guarding toys on a shelf.

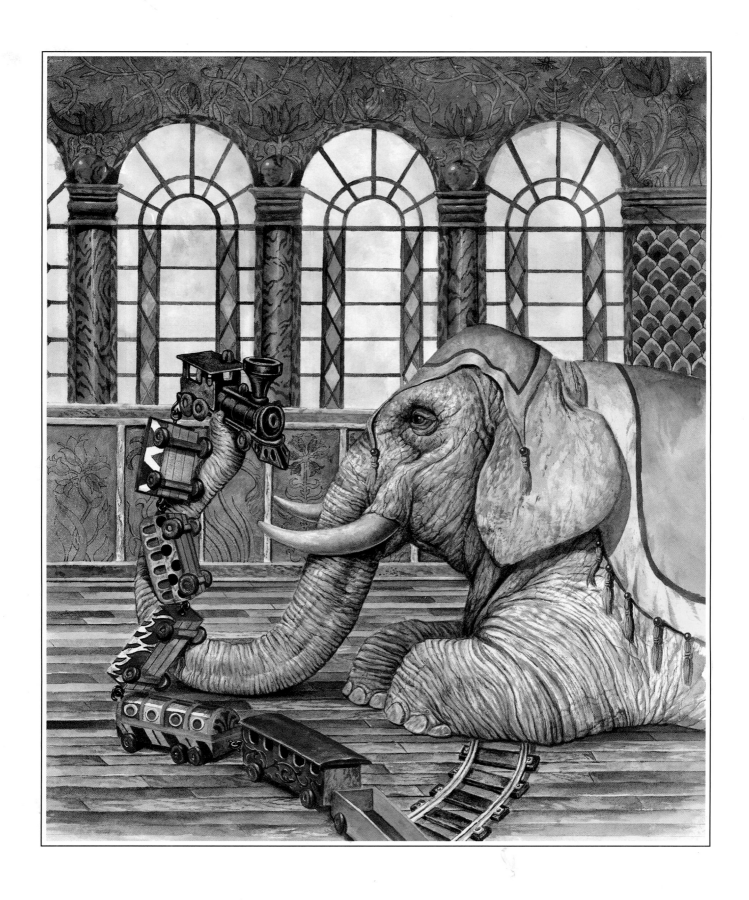

E is for Elephant,
on the right track.

F is for Frog,
who never looks back.

G is for Giraffe,
minding a tray.

H is for Hippo,
preparing to play.

I is for Ibis,
arranging some pears.

J is for Jaguar,
checking the stairs.

K is for Kingfisher,
the best in the box.

L is for Lion,
styling his locks.

M is for Mandrill,
expecting a call.

N is for Narwhal,
wrapped in a shawl.

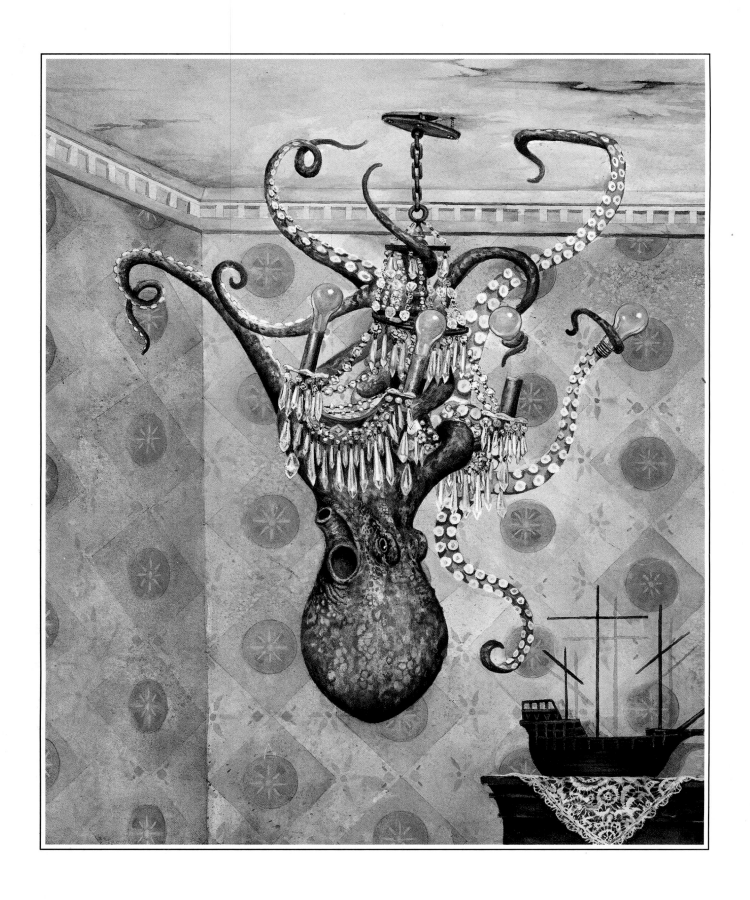

O is for Octopus,
changing a light.

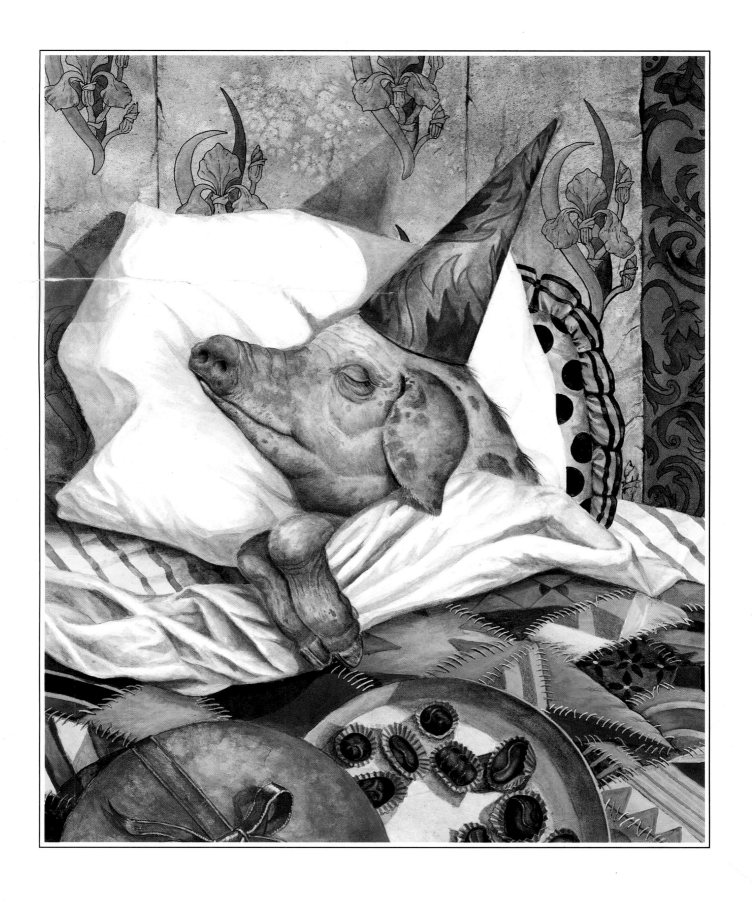

P is for Pig,
tucked in for the night.

Q is for Quetzal,
decorating with flowers.

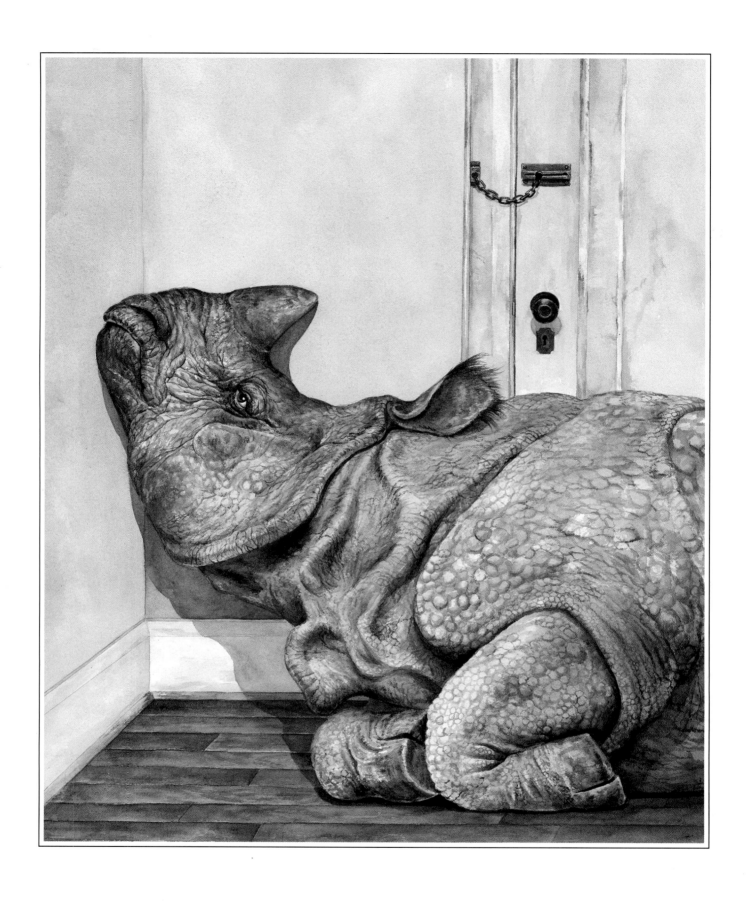

R is for Rhino,
daydreaming for hours.

S is for Swan,
dancing with glee.

T is for Tarantula,
arriving for tea.

U is for Unicorn,
the shyest of beasts.

V is for Vulture,
dying to feast.

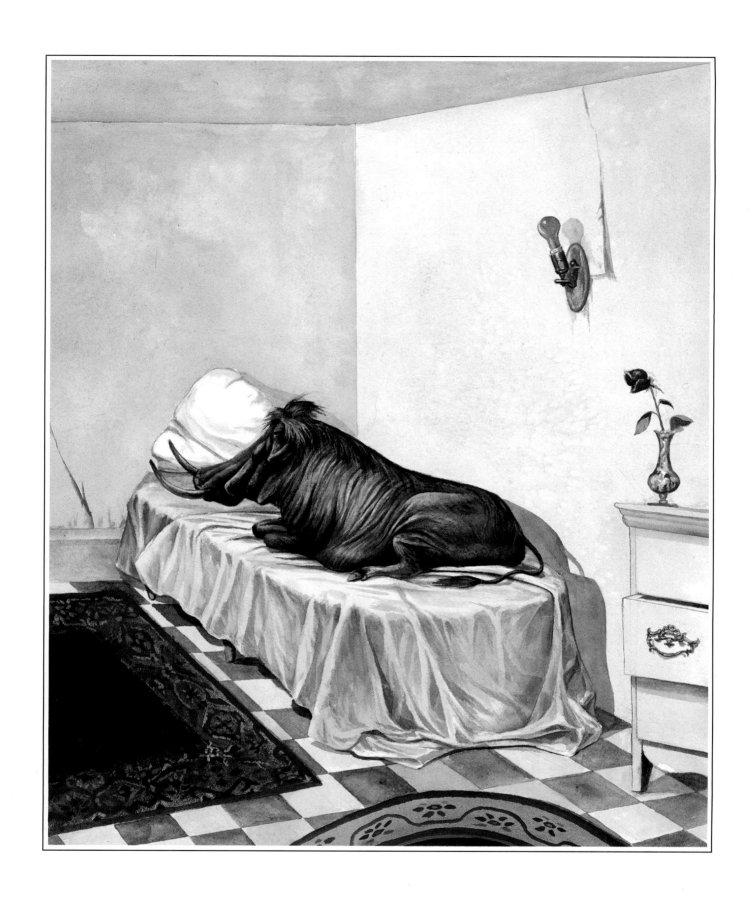

W is for Warthog,
feeling under the weather.

X is for Xenosaur,
composing a letter.

Y is for Yak,
seeking a path.

Z is for Zebra,
taking a bath.